So You Want To Learn:
JUGGLING

MATTHEW WALL

For the clumsy kid in us all

Handersen Publishing, LLC
Lincoln, Nebraska

Copyright © 2017 Matthew Wall

Library of Congress Control Number: 2017933247

Handersen Publishing, LLC, Lincoln, Nebraska

ISBN-13: 978-1941429570

Publisher Website: www.handersenpublishing.com
Publisher Email: editors@handersenpublishing.com

SO...
YOU
WANT TO
JUGGLE

WHAT YOU WILL NEED

A set of juggling balls

If you don't have juggling balls, three of anything will work. Make sure they have a similar weight, size and balance.

3

Remember how I just said grab three of anything? Well, there is one exception…

ABSOLUTELY NO EGGS!

Now you have everything
you will need to start.

READY...

1 2 3 JUGGLE!

OK, THAT DIDN'T GO SO WELL…

L et's back up a step or two and take a look at some juggling basics before we attempt to juggle three balls again.

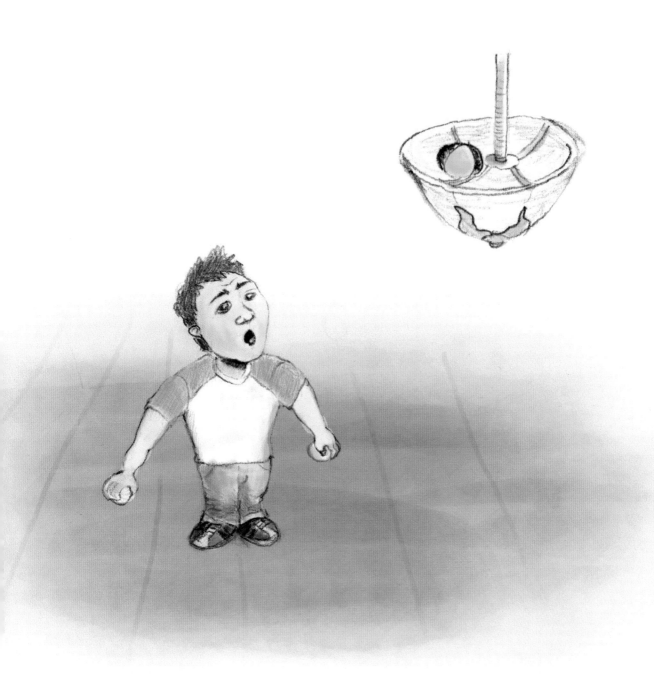

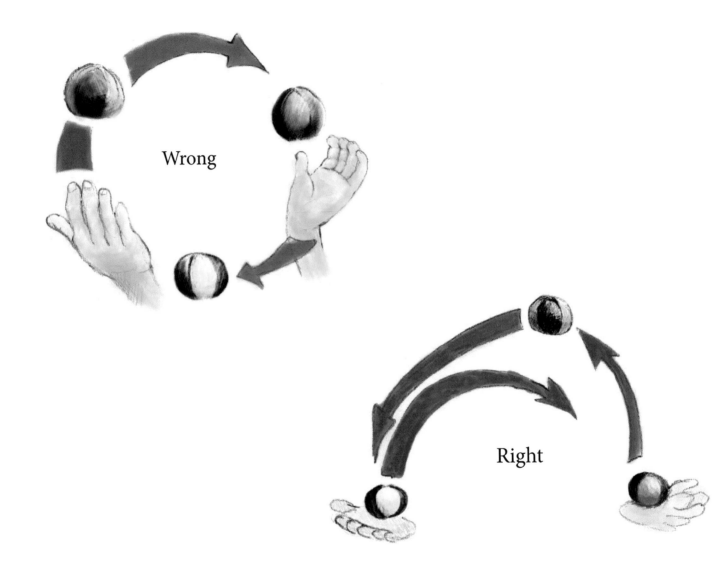

Wrong

Right

8

CONTRARY TO POPULAR BELIEF

When you juggle, the balls do not travel around in a circular pattern. The objects travel in more of a criss-cross pattern. You will learn how to do this with a few simple exercises.

Exercise one:
the TOSS.
(easy peasy)

Start off with one ball in your right hand. Make a sweeping "J" like motion and toss the ball in a high arc that lands in your empty hand.

Your right hand will then move back to its original position. Be sure to practice tossing the ball back in the other direction. Repeat this exercise until it feels natural.

This probably won't take very long.

10

EXERCISE TWO:
THE DOUBLE TOSS.
(GETTING HARDER)

This time start with two balls, one in each hand. Using the motion you learned in exercise one, toss the ball in your right hand. When it reaches the top of its arc, toss the ball in your left hand. Again, repeat this exercise until it feels natural.

This might take a while.

EXERCISE THREE:
REWIRE your BRAIN.
(NOT IMPOSSIBLE)

Now it's time to move on to three balls. Once you can do this, you will officially be juggling!

Start with two balls in your right hand and one in the left. Toss one of the balls in your right hand. When it reaches the top of its arc, toss the ball in your left hand.

When the second ball reaches the top of its arc, toss the last ball in your right hand.

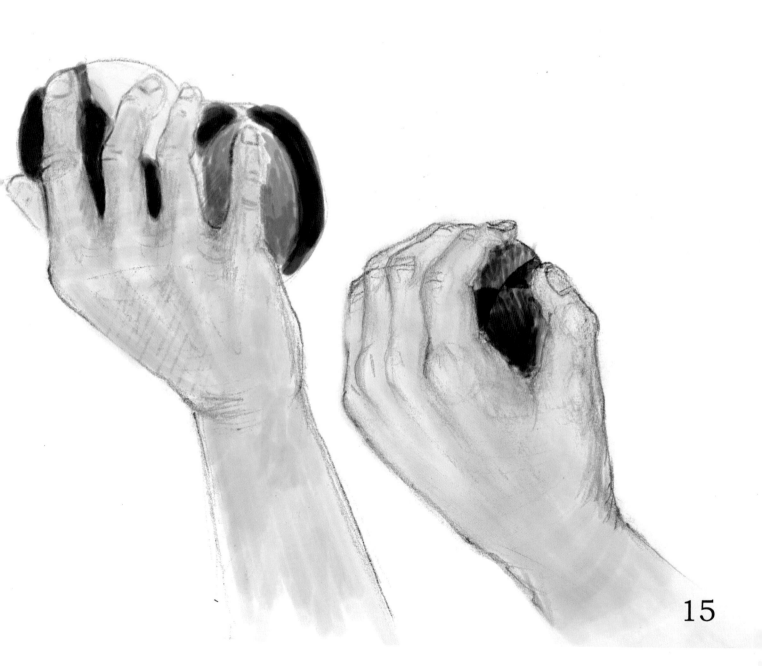

15

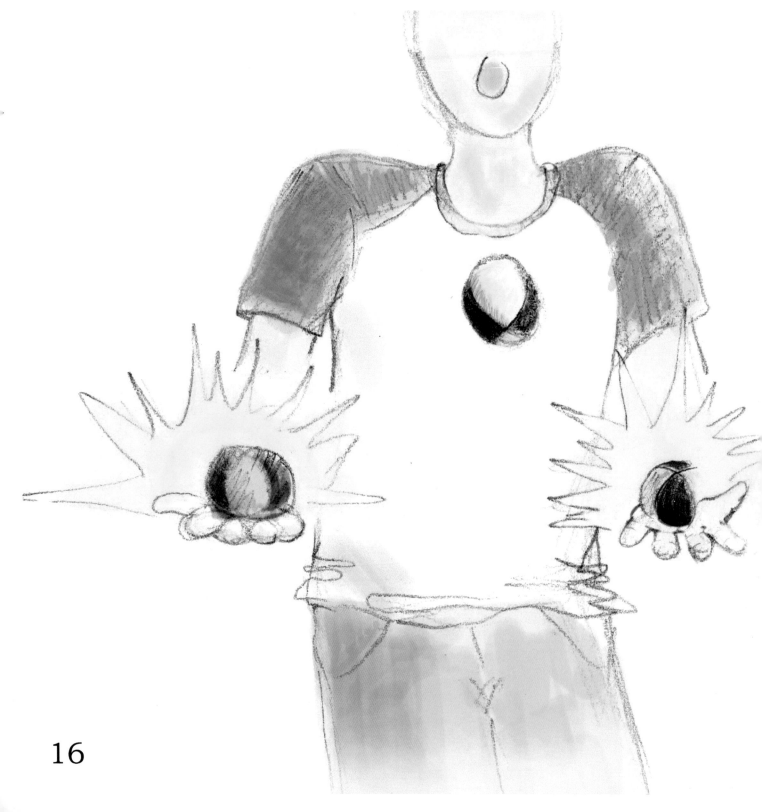

THIS IS WHERE YOUR BRAIN IMPLODES.

Both hands are full, and now you have to catch the ball that is in the air.

The automatic reaction is to drop what's in your hands to catch the airborne ball.

The other reaction you might have is to try to "shovel-pass" the ball in your left hand to catch the ball in the air.

THIS NEVER WORKS.

19

HANG IN THERE!

Keep practicing. Eventually you _will_ get it. And before long, you will be juggling with the best of them!

But remember, even after you become a juggling master...

ABSOLUTELY NO EGGS!

It's TIME TO REVIEW. READY...

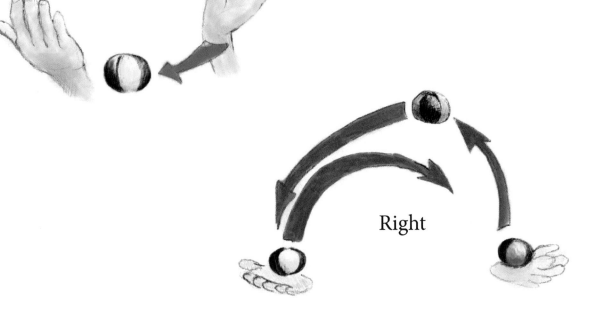

Wrong

Right

- Start with two balls in your right hand and one in the left.

- Toss one of the balls in your right hand. When it reaches the top of its arc, toss the ball in your left hand.

- When the second ball reaches the top of its arc, toss the last ball in your right hand.

NOW YOU'RE JUGGLING!

Matthew Wall has been juggling since he was nine years old. He also enjoys playing the guitar, photography and hanging out with his amazing, beautiful, talented wife, Shannon at their home in Gainesville, Florida.

This is his first picture book, although you may have seen a few of his illustrations in Stinkwaves Magazine.

Discover more at www.handersenpublishing.com

Handersen Publishing LLC
Great books for young readers
www.handersenpublishing.com

Handersen Publishing, LLC is an independent publishing house. If you enjoyed this book please consider leaving a review on Amazon or Goodreads. A little review can be a big help for the little guys!

Printed in Great Britain
by Amazon